The LOUDEST, FASTEST, BEST Drummer in Kansas

by Marguerite W. Davol ★ illustrated by Cat Bowman Smith

Orchard Books New York

*To my sister Ora Mae, and to the
memory of our big sister Maggie*
—M.W.D.

*To all children who have endured
the dark forces of nature*
—C.B.S.

Orchard Books, A Grolier Company
95 Madison Avenue, New York, NY 10016

Manufactured in the United States of America
Printed and bound by Phoenix Color Corp.
Book design by Zara Design
The text of this book is set in 14 point Caslon.
The illustrations are gouache.

10 9 8 7 6 5 4 3 2 1

Library of Congress Cataloging-in-Publication Data
Davol, Marguerite W.
The loudest, fastest, best drummer in Kansas / by Marguerite W. Davol ;
illustrated by Cat Bowman Smith.   p.   cm.
Summary: Maggie saves the town of Serena, Kansas, with her loud, fast drumming.
ISBN 0-531-30191-5 (trade : alk. paper).—ISBN 0-531-33191-1 (library : alk. paper)
[1. Drum Fiction. 2. Tall tales.] I. Smith, Cat Bowman, ill. II. Title.
PZ7.D32155Lo   2000   [E]—dc21   99-29513

Welcome to Serena, the home of Maggie, the best drummer in Kansas. You can bet everybody around here knows Maggie. Yep, knows all about how she was a born drummer. Some people think it was because of that dratted woodpecker's *tat-a-tat-tat* outside her mama's window before Maggie was born. But old Doc Acton blames the Fourth of July parade. Led by the Kansas Drum and Bugle Corps, that parade marched past the Serena Hospital at the exact moment Maggie was born—*Boom, ta-ra, ta-ra, Boom.*

Now old Doc Acton was the first to discover Maggie was a drummer. He's told that story over and over—about how that tiny baby reached up and grabbed his stethoscope! He claims she began beating on his chest—*pum-pa, pum-pa, pum-pa*—in perfect rhythm with her heartbeat . . . and with the bass drum in the Kansas Drum and Bugle Corps.

Of course her mama knew right away that Maggie was a born drummer. She still tells about how Maggie drummed on her crib at night—*Plup-a-plup-plan.* That baby drummed so much that all the boards popped apart—*ker-Blam-blum!*

"Stop, Maggie," Mama would groan. "Oh, my aching ears!"

But did Maggie stop? Nope! She just crawled over, picked up the crib slats, and kept right on drumming on the floor.

Mealtimes, Maggie banged spoons on her high chair—*clang-a-clong-clung*—until she wore a hole clean through it. And then, when she could walk, Maggie grabbed anything she could find: pencils or pie plates, hairbrushes or hot dogs—yep, hot dogs!—and beat a *clickety-thickety* rhythm on every window and door in the house. She *whop-whapped* on walls, drummed up and down stairs, *whang-banged* on pans, and tap-danced the chairs.

Day after day, Mama would moan, "Stop, Maggie. My aching ears!"

But did Maggie stop? No way! She just kept on drumming.

When Maggie was nearly six, she begged, "A drum, Mama. I need a drum.
Brumm, brumm. A real drum."

Looking around her banged-up, beat-on house, Mama finally gave in.
Maggie's birthday present that year was a set of real drums. Picking up the
drumsticks, she announced, "I'm going to be the loudest, fastest, best drummer
in the State of Kansas!"

Mama could only shake her head and mutter, "I believe it."

Maggie practiced every day, all day. Loud riffs and drumrolls bounced off the walls—*Bling-ingg, Bling-ingg*. Mama threw up her hands when the noise curdled the milk and cracked all the eggs, shriveled the onions and peeled the oranges. Worse, the bread Mama kneaded refused to rise.

"You've got to stop, Maggie," Mama demanded. "Oh, my aching ears!"

But did Maggie stop? Of course not! She just took her drums outdoors.

You could see Maggie strutting up and down Main Street, left-right, left-right, drumming. Loudly. *Brumpty-brum, bing-bang-bung*. Soon the squirrels quit chewing holes in attics, and the mice quit chewing holes in cheese. Ears quivering, they slunk away. Even the rats left town. As for the citizens of Serena, did they leave? Nope! They just grumbled, "Stop now, Maggie. Oh, our aching ears!"

Well, if you can imagine it, each day Maggie's drumming grew even louder, LOUDER!—*Bang! CRASH!*—as she shouted in rhythm with her drums, "I'm going to be the loudest, fastest, best drummer in Kansas!"

In fact, she drummed so loudly that sidewalks sank and windows shattered. Sweeping up glass, folks in town shook their heads. What could anyone do about a born drummer, anyway? They just groaned, "Oh, our aching ears!"

The sign on the desk reads:

At the Town Council
An ordinance
must be passed
stating
FROM NOW ON,
DRUMMING IS
AGAINST
THE LAW.
Mayor Plogg

MAYOR PLOGG

And then, on the day Maggie worked up to a full drumroll—*brrooommm*—
the roof of the Town Hall jiggled three inches to the right . . . then three inches
to the left. . . . Mayor Plogg, looking up at the ceiling of his office, was furious.
He declared, "Born drummer or not, that girl's gotta be stopped!" And he had the
Serena Town Council pass an ordinance: "From now on, drumming is against
the law."

In just one day, Serena looked like it had come down with the measles.
Anti-drumming posters were plastered everywhere. Mayor Plogg even ordered the
chief of police to impound Maggie's drums.

But did Maggie stop? No! And did the chief of police confiscate Maggie's drums? No way! Because here's what happened the very next morning. People walking outdoors heard a faint *zingg*, which grew louder—*ZZZinggg, ZZZINggg*—and louder—*ZZZINGGG, ZZZINGGG*. A squadron of killer wasps had invaded Serena! Panicking, the people pushed into the Town Hall. "Do something!" they demanded of Mayor Plogg.

Before the mayor could open his mouth, another sound was heard over the winging whine of the attacking wasps. *Brumm, brumm. Brumm, brumm.* The rumble and roll grew louder and louder, the loudest folks had ever heard—*Brumm-brumm-brammity-BRUMM, BRUMM, BRUMM.* Maggie came marching down the street, drumsticks flying, yelling "Look out, wasps!"

When those killer wasps met Maggie's drumroll, they struggled to push past that enormous wall of sound. But one by one, each wasp's stinger began to bend until—*Snap! Snap! Snap-snap! Snap!* Why, it rained so many stingers, the piles were as high as a cow's eyebrows. Mayor Plogg had to call out the Highway Department to bulldoze all those stingers off Main Street.

After that, the townspeople didn't complain—at least, not much—about Maggie's drumming. They simply stuffed cotton in their ears and muttered, "Oh, our blocked-up ears!"

Only Mayor Plogg continued to grumble. "We've passed a law. Drumming is forbidden. Now we gotta enforce it," he told every man and woman he met. But with all that cotton in their ears, who could hear him? So Maggie kept on drumming.

Then one day the drumming got so loud it shattered Mayor Plogg's office door—the glass one with his name spelled out in fancy script. He yelled, "That did it!"

Charging down Main Street, hands pressed against his ears, Mayor Plogg came up behind Maggie, who was marching left-right, left-right, as usual. He screeched, "STOP. NO DRUMMING. IT'S ILLEGAL!"

Of course Maggie couldn't hear him, which only made Mayor Plogg angrier. He tried to grab Maggie's drum, but that bad-tempered mayor stumbled and fell smack into her bass drum—*sploomf!* Well, *that* made Maggie stop! She had to tug and pull to get the mayor out. And it wasn't easy.

Red-faced, Mayor Plogg roared, "I'll have you arrested. Put in jail for disturbing the peace."

Now Serena doesn't even have a jail, but Maggie sure didn't want to be arrested. She stopped marching up and down Main Street. Instead, Maggie stayed in her room staring out the window. She tried drumming slowly, softly—*tlink, a-tlankity, tlunk*—while watching a lone spider spin its web in time with the soft beat. But finally Maggie put aside her drums. "Now I'll never be the loudest, fastest, best drummer in Kansas," she said sadly.

For the rest of that
summer, Serena, Kansas, was quiet.
Very quiet. Too quiet! Folks were startled to
hear a meadowlark sing and jumped at the sound
of wind rustling in the wheat fields. Why, it was so
quiet that in the orchards you could hear worms
boring into apples, then spitting out the peel.
Chunggg, pi-too! Squirrels chittered in attics
again, and mice scrabbled in cellars.
Even the rats scurried back.

The last Thursday of August was hot, the hottest day anyone, even old Doc Acton, could remember. Corn shriveled in the fields and silos slumped. Fire hydrants spouted steam. Why, it was so hot, kids stuck to the sidewalks! Their mamas had to pry their sneakers loose with crowbars—*ker-shpluck!*

Then along about four o'clock, a dark storm cloud loomed in the west. People got scared, watching that cloud pile up higher and higher, twisting and turning as it grew. A humongous tornado began to roar right toward the center of Serena—*ZZrrOOmm, ZZrrOOmm*—with a sound louder than a dozen trains, louder than a hundred planes.

Frantic, the townspeople dashed for shelter, shouting "Call the police! The Fire Department! Get Mayor Plogg!" But could anyone be heard above the roar of that storm? No! No one. The tornado snaked along Main Street, twisting lamp-posts into corkscrews and tossing mailboxes like Frisbees, letters streaming from box after box. Then that funnel-shaped cloud sucked up all the squirrels, mice, and rats—*schlurrp*—whirled them around, and whisked them off to Missouri!

Believe it or not, that tornado picked up the roof of the Town Hall, spinning it around and around like a merry-go-round—without horses. As the roof rotated, Mayor Plogg was yanked right out of his office and swallowed up by the tremendous twister! It sure looked like the mayor, along with the whole town of Serena, would be whooshed away to Missouri too! However . . .

About that time, Maggie looked out her window and saw the twister. For a second, she hesitated. "No drumming," Mayor Plogg had ordered. But Maggie knew what she had to do. Yelling "Whoopie, wait for me!," Maggie grabbed her drum and rushed out of her house.

Within moments, another sound could be heard above the roar of the whirling storm. Louder than *two* dozen trains, louder than *two* hundred planes, louder than the threatening tornado, in fact *twice* as loud as she'd ever drummed before, Maggie came marching to meet the storm. *BOOM, BROOOM-BROOM, BAMMITY, BRAGGITY, BOOM!* "Look out, tornado!" she shouted.

The deafening, ear-throbbing drum beat fast, faster. Loud, louder, the LOUDEST sound ever heard in Kansas! In rhythm with Maggie's drum, the twisting storm turned fast, faster, fastest, a blur against the sky. And then—can't you picture it?—that tornado began to break apart, whirling itself to death in time with Maggie's drumbeat. Flecks of cloud went flying every which way, harmless little puffs in the sky, until the entire twister disappeared.

And as the storm split apart, the Town Hall roof stopped spinning and settled down right into place. What about Mayor Plogg? He plopped onto a soft flower bed right next to the Town Hall. Only his dignity—and the marigolds—were squashed.

The sky cleared, and Maggie's drumbeats became slower and slower, softer and softer, until they were little puffs of sound. *Pit-it, pit-it. Pit-it, pit-it.* The huge sound faded to silence. For a few moments, not a wisp or a whisper could be heard. Then, led by Maggie's proud mama, a most tremendous noise filled the streets of Serena. The whole town—even Mayor Plogg—shouted and cheered. "Yea, Maggie! You are the loudest, fastest, best drummer in the State of Kansas."

Everyone yelled so loud, in fact, that the roof on the Town Hall popped up three inches on the right—and it's stayed that way to this day! Here in Serena, you can't miss that cockeyed roof right in the center of town.

And Maggie? You can still hear her drumming up and down Main Street every day from one to three—*Brroom, bang, wham, whang, BOOM!* The rest of the time, the loudest noise in town is the drumming of raindrops on the crooked Town Hall roof.